FLY HIGH, FLY GUY!

Tedd Arnold

Cartwheel
·B·O·O·K·S·®

SCHOLASTIC INC.
New York   Toronto   London   Auckland
Sydney   Mexico City   New Delhi   Hong Kong

For Christene
—T.A.

Library of Congress Cataloging-in-Publication Data:
Arnold, Tedd.
 Fly high, fly guy! / by Tedd Arnold.
    p. cm.
 "Cartwheel books."
 Summary: When Buzz, his parents, and his pet fly go on a road trip and get lost, Fly Guy comes to the
rescue to help them find their way home.
 ISBN 978-0-545-00722-1
 [1. Flies--Fiction. 2. Automobile travel--Fiction.] I. Title.
PZ7.A7379Ro 2008
[E]—dc22   2007005317
                            ISBN 978-0-545-00722-1

29 28 27   18 19 20

                    Printed in the U.S.A. 88
                    First printing, May 2008

A boy had a pet fly.
He named him Fly Guy.
Fly Guy could say
the boy's name—

Chapter 1

One day Buzz said,
"It's time to take
a road trip."

ly Guy wanted to go, too.

He's too little," said Mom.

He might get lost."

"Sorry," said Dad.
"Fly Guy stays home."

He shut the trunk.
"Okay, let's hit the road!"

The family drove and drove

They stopped for a picnic.
Mom opened the trunk.
Fly Guy flew out.

Dad said, "How did
he get in there?"

"Just don't lose him,"
said Mom and Dad.
"Now, let's eat!"

Chapter 2

They drove to the beach.

MOTEL

Then it was time to go.
Mom and Dad said,
"Is Fly Guy lost?"

"No," said Buzz.
"Here he is!"

They drove to
the art museum.

KISS

Then it was time to go.
Mom and Dad said,
"Is Fly Guy lost?"

"No," said Buzz.
"Here he is!"

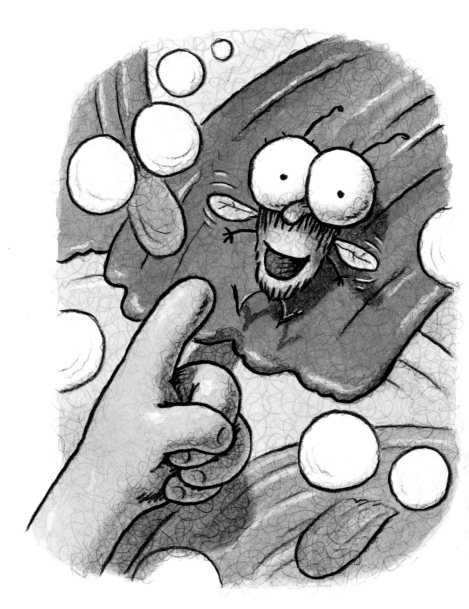

They drove to
the fun park.

Then it was time to go.
Mom and Dad said,
"Is Fly Guy lost?"

"No," said Buzz.
"Here he is!"

Chapter 3

"It's time to go home,"
said Mom.
"Let's hit the road,"
said Dad.

They drove

and drove

and drove

and drove

and drove

and drove

and drove

and drove

and drove

and drove

and drove

and drove

and drove

But they did not get home.
"We're lost," said Mom
and Dad.

Buzz and Fly Guy had an idea.
Buzz said, "Fly high, Fly Guy!"

Fly Guy flew high into the sky.
He used his super fly eyes
to spy their house.

Fly Guy led the way home.

"Thank you, Fly Guy,"
said Mom and Dad.
"You saved the day!
Yay, Fly Guy!"